Blossom and Beany

Beany the duck was diving for insects when the little piglet burst through the hedge and splashed down on top of him. Beany flapped his wings madly and turned himself right way up. "Watch out!" he spluttered.

Blossom
and Beany

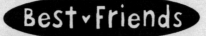

Best Friends

Blossom and Beany

by Jenny Dale
Illustrated by Susan Hellard

SCHOLASTIC INC.

New York   Toronto   London   Auckland   Sydney
Mexico City   New Delhi   Hong Kong   Buenos Aires

ISBN 0-439-66991-X

12 11 10 9 8 7 6 5 4 3   6 7 8 9/0

Printed in the U.S.A.   40
First Scholastic Printing, November 2004

Special thanks to Stephanie Baudet

Chapter one

"Wait for me!" Blossom squealed.

"No! You're too small to play with us," grunted her biggest brother. He twitched his curly tail and scampered off.

Blossom was the smallest piglet in the litter. She watched her eleven brothers and sisters run to the other end of the field. They squeaked happily as they began to play a game of chase.

Blossom wished she could join them. She looked down at her little legs. What her brother said was true. She couldn't run as fast as they could. She wished she knew how to grow more quickly. She ate just as much as they did.

"It's not fair," she snuffled. "I never have anyone to play with." Her ears drooped sadly, and her tail lost its curl. Blossom stomped across the field, hoping to find a place to play on her own. She came to the thick hedge, but that didn't stop her. She pushed her way through. As she popped out on the other side, her feet skidded out from under her. With a surprised squeal, Blossom slipped into a deep and muddy puddle.

Beany the duck was diving for insects when the little piglet burst through the hedge and splashed down on top of him. Beany flapped his wings madly and

turned himself right way up. "Watch out!" he spluttered.

"Sorry," Blossom grunted. "I didn't mean to sink you." Blossom looked down and saw that she was covered in mud. Water was dripping off her ears.

"Don't worry, I'm not *that* easy to sink," Beany quacked cheerfully. "But what are you doing in my puddle? Why aren't you playing with the other piglets?"

Blossom hung her head. Her ears flopped forward and nearly covered her eyes.

"I'm too small," she grunted. "They won't let me play with them because I can't keep up." She looked at Beany. "My name's Blossom, by the way."

"I'm Beany," quacked the friendly duck. He swam to the edge of the puddle and stepped out. Then he shook himself, showering Blossom with water.

Blossom gave a little squeal. "Where do you live?" she grunted.

"In the farmyard," Beany replied. "Have you ever been there?"

Blossom shook her head. "I've never been farther than this puddle," she snuffled.

"Why don't you come back with me?" Beany suggested. "You can meet my friends. Besides, I'm hungry. If we hurry, we'll be back in time for lunch."

Blossom thought for a moment. She looked at Beany's short legs. She would certainly be able to keep up with *him*! She nodded her head and twitched her curly

tail. She'd never been to the farmyard. Not even her brothers and sisters had been that far.

Beany gave himself another shake and began to waddle across the field.

"Why don't you fly, Beany?" Blossom grunted, trotting after him.

Beany stopped. His head drooped. "I *like* walking," he quacked. "Come on, follow me."

Blossom walked beside him. She had to walk quite slowly. This time, *she* was the one with the longer legs.

But when they reached the end of the field, Blossom's heart sank. A gate! She looked at the thick wooden bars. The gaps between them were very narrow. "I can't get through," she grunted.

Beany looked at her with his round black eyes. "Squeeze underneath," he replied. "You're not very big. I'm sure you could if you tried."

Blossom trotted up to the gate and pushed her snout through. There were lots of exciting smells. She really *did* want to explore the farmyard.

She crouched down and tried to push her body under the bottom bar. The ground felt gritty under her tummy, and the bar scraped her back.

Blossom grunted and wriggled and pushed with her back feet. And then she was through! "I did it, Beany!" she squealed.

"Good job!" Beany quacked, flapping his wings happily. "Sometimes being small is a good thing." Then he gave a loud squawk. "Oh, dear!"

Blossom looked up. In his excitement, Beany had flown up in the air. He was now perched on top of the gate — but he was wobbling from side to side. As Blossom watched, Beany lost his balance and fell!

chapter Two

"Look out!" Blossom squealed.

Too late! Beany sailed through the air and landed with a thump on the path. He scrambled to his feet and shook his dusty feathers.

"Beany! Are you all right?" Blossom snuffled.

"Of course I am!" Beany quacked. He looked a bit embarrassed. "Come on. It's not far now." He ran off up the track, wings flapping.

Blossom had to trot to catch up with

him. "Wait, Beany!" she puffed. "Why didn't you just fly over the gate? Ducks can fly, can't they?"

Beany stopped and looked down at his feet. "Yes," he quacked sadly. "Ducks can fly. But I'm not very good at it. You see, I'm afraid of heights."

Blossom looked at him in surprise. "But you're a duck! How can you be scared of heights?"

Beany didn't answer. Blossom nudged him with her snout, to show she didn't mind. Side by side, they walked along the soft, sandy track to the farmyard.

Beany led the way across the yard, around the pond, and over to the big barn. He couldn't wait to reach the food bin. He hadn't eaten anything for hours.

In the doorway of the barn, he stopped and looked around. Now *where* was that piglet?

Blossom was standing in the corner of the farmyard, staring at the pond. "What a *huge* puddle!" she squealed. It seemed to stretch away forever, and lots and lots of birds were swimming around on it.

Beany quacked with laughter and waddled back to Blossom. "It's not a puddle. It's a duck pond," he replied.

A whole flock of birds flew off the pond and gathered around Blossom. She felt a bit nervous. Some of them were much bigger than she.

"These are my brothers and sisters," Beany quacked, waving his wing at four ducks. "The big white birds with long

necks are geese. They can be a little un-
friendly sometimes. If they hiss at you,
keep out of their way!"

Blossom looked warily at the geese. She
didn't want to be hissed at.

Suddenly, there was a loud *WOOF*! All
the birds scattered, squawking loudly and
flapping their wings.

Tickly feathers brushed Blossom's face and made her blink. She let out a squeal.

"Don't worry, that's only Ruff, the sheepdog," quacked Beany. But his voice sounded quiet and far away. Blossom looked around. Beany was floating in the middle of the pond with all the other ducks!

Blossom jumped as a huge black-and-white dog came bounding up, wagging his tail. "Hello!" he woofed. "You're very small for a pig."

"I'm a pigLET," Blossom snorted angrily. She wished everyone would stop saying how small she was! "I'll grow."

Beany bobbed on the duck pond and watched Blossom stamp her foot at Ruff. He could see that Blossom was not afraid.

The barn door opened, and Mrs. Brown, the farmer's wife, walked out. She was carrying a big bowl of corn.

"Lunchtime!" quacked all the birds, flapping and splashing toward her.

Beany rushed out of the pond and hurried over to Blossom. "You'd better hide," he quacked. "You don't want to be sent back to your field just yet."

Blossom nodded and trotted behind a bucket. Beany could just see her pink snout poking out from one side and her curly tail from the other.

A sound like noisy raindrops made him turn around. Mrs. Brown was scooping corn out of the bowl and throwing it onto the ground. Yum! Beany flapped his wings and ran over as fast as he could.

When Mrs. Brown went back inside the farmhouse, Blossom crept out from behind the bucket and trotted over to Beany. She sniffed the ground hopefully.

Beany looked up at her, surprised. "Oh, no, Blossom!" he cried. "Are you hungry?" He looked around. The ground was already quite bare! All the corn had been eaten.

For a moment, Beany felt bad, but then he had an idea. "Come on," he quacked. "I'll show you where the corn bin is. It's in the barn with the monster."

"W-What monster?" asked Blossom, feeling a bit worried.

But Beany didn't reply. He had already disappeared inside the barn. Mrs. Brown had left the door slightly open.

Blossom hurried to catch up with Beany and squeezed through the door into the cool, dark building.

"There it is," quacked Beany, pointing with his wing. "It's been asleep ever since it got here yesterday."

Blossom stared. A big yellow monster stood at the other end of the barn. Feeling very brave, Blossom walked a little bit

nearer and gazed up at its shiny round eyes. The monster didn't move.

"Over here, Blossom!" quacked Beany. He scrambled up onto a long feed bin. "You'll have to get the lid off first." He jumped down again and looked hopefully at Blossom.

Blossom heaved her front feet up and

rested them against the trough. Then she wriggled her snout under the lid and pushed hard.

Nothing happened.

She tried again. The lid moved a tiny bit.

"Push!" shouted Beany.

Blossom heaved once more. Suddenly, the lid flipped off and clattered to the floor.

The noise made some of the other ducks pop their heads around the door. "Hooray!" they quacked. "Blossom took the lid off the corn bin!"

"Dig in, everyone," Beany quacked. He fluttered up onto the rim of the trough and dipped his beak into the tasty corn.

Blossom dug her snout into the feed bin. The corn was almost as good as her pig food!

Suddenly, the door was flung open. A beam of sunlight spread across the barn floor.

"What's going on in here?" said a stern voice.

"Look out! It's Mrs. Brown!" quacked Beany.

All the ducks quickly scrambled out of the trough and fluttered to the ground, showering kernels of corn everywhere.

Mrs. Brown looked very angry. She shooed the ducks out the door.

Blossom stood beside the trough and watched them leave. Her tummy was too full now for her to run away.

Mrs. Brown gently picked up Blossom and tucked the piglet under her arm. "You're a long way from home," she said.

"You naughty girl! Let's get you back to your field where you belong."

As Mrs. Brown carried her out of the barn, Blossom saw Beany pushing his way out of a huddle of ducks.

"Bye, Blossom!" he quacked. "See you in the puddle tomorrow!"

Blossom twitched her snout to show she understood.

Mrs. Brown carried her along the sandy lane to her field. "There you are, piglet," she said, putting her on the ground. "No more straying, or you'll get lost."

Feeling full and tired, Blossom lay down in the sun and shut her eyes.

The next thing Blossom knew, someone was prodding her in the ribs.

"Come on, lazybones!" squealed one of her sisters. "It's time for supper."

"I am *not* lazy!" Blossom protested. "I've had a very busy day. I met a duck called Beany, and he took me to the farmyard. . . ."

Her brothers and sisters stopped eating and turned to look at her.

"You're dreaming," grunted her second biggest brother.

"You're too scared to go beyond the gate!" squealed her biggest sister.

"Well, I *did*," Blossom grunted. *She* knew it was all true! And she had gone *much* farther than *they* ever had!

chapter Three

The next morning, as usual, Blossom's brothers and sisters scampered off to play at the other end of the field. But today Blossom didn't mind being left behind at all. Beany was coming to play with her!

As soon as the other piglets were out of sight, Blossom trotted to the puddle in the next field.

But Beany wasn't there. The puddle was empty.

"Oh, no!" Blossom snuffled. "Where

are you, Beany?" She lay down in the
cool water, feeling very disappointed.

A few minutes later, Beany waddled
into the field. He hoped Blossom would
be waiting for him. He had some exciting
news for her!

Beany spotted the piglet, fast asleep in
the puddle. Only her snout was above the
water! He jumped in and swam over to

her, splashing her with his wings. "Wake up, Blossom!" he quacked.

Blossom scrambled to her feet. Drops of muddy water flew all over Beany's feathers. "Where have you been?" she squealed. "I've been waiting for *hours!*"

Beany tutted and carefully shook all the water off his wings. "Guess what happened at the farm this morning!" he said. "The big monster woke up! It's gone down to the field near the river. One of the ducks followed it all the way. He said it's gobbling up all the wheat in the field. It must be *really* hungry!"

He opened his beady eyes very wide. "All the ducks have flown off to look," he went on. "And some of the geese went, too." Then his wings drooped and he looked very sad. "But I've never been to the river. It's such a long way to walk."

Blossom felt very sorry for him. Then she had an idea. She wanted to see the hungry monster, too. She and Beany could go together!

She scrambled out of the puddle. "I'll come with you!" she squealed. "The walk won't seem so long if we go together. Which way is it to the river?"

"Back past the duck pond," quacked Beany, sounding very excited. "Come on! We're off on a monster hunt!"

chapter four

Blossom wriggled under the gate and followed Beany back up the lane.

They went through the farmyard, where the pond lay silent and empty. Everyone had gone to see the monster.

Beany led Blossom down a path with tall hedges on either side.

"Are you sure this is the right way?" Blossom grunted.

"Oh, yes," quacked Beany. "I saw the other birds flying this way."

Suddenly, Blossom stopped and pricked up her ears. "Listen!" she squealed.

There was a faint rumbling noise in the distance. It got louder and louder.

"It's the monster!" Beany quacked. He flapped his wings and waddled at top speed around the corner to a gate. On the other side of the gate was a huge field of golden wheat. Growling and roaring, the monster came into sight.

"There it is!" Blossom squealed.

Beany hopped up and down. "Look out! It's coming toward us." He dodged under the hedge and peeped out.

The monster rattled past, gobbling up the wheat and leaving behind a wide path of bitten-off stalks.

"Wow!" Blossom whispered fearfully.

"It *is* a hungry monster! I hope it doesn't eat us up, too!" She pushed her way under the hedge, into the next field. Then she ran and ran.

The grass was very tall, and Blossom couldn't see where she was going. Beany, with his long neck, could just see over the grass.

"Turn right!" he puffed. "We're nearly at the river."

All of a sudden, the long grass stopped and Blossom tumbled out onto a wide green path. Beside the path was a river that sparkled and bubbled over a bed of pebbles. Blossom slithered down the muddy bank and paddled into the water. It was very cold! Little waves tickled her tummy and pulled at her legs.

Beany jumped in beside her. He bobbed along and swirled out of sight behind some big rocks. Blossom waded carefully after him, the sun warming her back.

Beany climbed out of the river and stood on the bank. He looked down at something on the grass. "Blossom!" he quacked. "I've found some food!"

Blossom scrambled up the bank. Her eyes opened very wide. A red blanket was spread out on the grass. On top of it were paper plates piled high with sandwiches and cakes. Blossom sniffed. They smelled really good. She stretched out her pink snout and picked up a sandwich.

Beany pecked at one of the cakes. A blob of something pink and gooey stuck to his bill. He angrily wiped it off onto the grass. "That's too sticky!" he quacked. He dug his beak into a sandwich instead. "Oh, good, it's sprouts and lettuce. My favorite!" he said as he happily took another bite.

Blossom couldn't answer because her mouth was too full. She pulled another sandwich off the plate.

"Hey!" There was a shout from farther down the bank.

"That's our picnic!" wailed another voice.

Blossom looked up in alarm. Three children were waving their arms and running toward her. This must be *their* food! She turned around to look for Beany, but he was already half flying, half running back the way they had come. Blossom dropped her sandwich and tore after him.

Beany splashed through the river and up the opposite bank. He crouched down and squeezed under a fence into a field.

Blossom wriggled through beside him and stopped, panting hard. "We were eating their picnic," she puffed. "No wonder they were mad."

"But it tasted yummy," Beany pointed out. His eyes shone with mischief.

Blossom looked around. "We didn't come this way," she grunted. "Do you know where we are?"

Beany stood up and shook his feathers. They couldn't be too far from the farm-yard, could they? "I'll go and have a look from the top of the field," he quacked, waddling off. His legs felt tired after their speedy escape. As he walked along, Beany began to feel worried. He didn't recognize that very tall tree over there. Or that thorny hedge . . .

Suddenly, Blossom squealed loudly. Beany turned around and squawked in alarm. A herd of black-and-white cows was heading straight for them!

chapter five

One of the cows loomed over Beany and put its nose very close to his face. He could feel its hot breath on his feathers. Beany didn't move a muscle. Did cows eat ducks? He didn't think so, but he still felt a bit scared.

"Who are you?" mooed the cow.

"I — I'm Beany," Beany quacked nervously.

Blossom felt worried about her friend. The cow looked enormous. "Go away!"

she squealed, stamping her front feet. "Leave Beany alone."

The cow turned its massive head and looked at Blossom. "You're in our field, little pig," it mooed.

"That's because we're lost," Blossom grunted bravely. "Can you tell us the way back to the farmyard?"

The cow shook its head and swished its

tail. "I've never been there," it mooed. It turned and walked slowly away from Beany.

"Come on, let's find our own way home," quacked Beany. But he still had no idea which way they had to go to get back to the farmyard. He looked up and down the field. It was no use. He just didn't know which way to go.

"What are we going to do?" Blossom wailed. Her ears drooped. Even her tail looked less curly.

Some pigeons flew overhead.

"Which way is it to the farmyard?" Beany called.

"Which way? This way! Which way? That way!" the pigeons cooed playfully. Then, with a quick flick of their wings, they swooped low over the hedge and they disappeared.

"Well, they weren't much help," Beany quacked. But at least the pigeons had given him an idea. "Maybe I could fly up and see where we are."

Blossom looked at Beany in surprise. It was a very good idea. If Beany flew as high as the trees, he could look down on the farm and figure out how to get home. But Beany was afraid of flying. And Blossom could see he already looked scared. She nudged him with her snout. "You'll be all right," she grunted. "If I could fly up there with you, I would, but pigs can't fly."

"It's okay. I know I have to fly one day," Beany replied bravely. He waddled over to the gate. His heart thumped with fear as he spread his wings and jumped. He flapped his wings madly, and he finally made it onto the top rail of the gate.

Beany paused and looked around. There was a small tree not far off. Maybe he should aim for that next. But it looked very high.

He pushed off the gate and flapped his wings as hard as he could. At first, he seemed to sink in the air. But he beat his wings faster and managed to land on a branch of the tree. He'd made it!

He glanced down at Blossom. She looked tiny. The ground looked so far away that it made Beany feel dizzy. For a moment he wobbled, then he took a deep breath. He had to keep going, or they would never get home. He spread his wings really wide and took off. A gentle breeze lifted him up, higher and higher. He swooped in lazy circles until he was above the treetops. Flying was easy!

From far below, Beany heard Blossom squeal. He gazed around. Everything looked very different from up here. He narrowed his eyes. There was the roof of the farmhouse! There was the duck pond. And there was the monster, fast asleep in the empty field of wheat.

Best of all, Beany could see the sandy path that led through the fields, all the way back to the farmyard. He swooped down and landed with a bit of a thud right beside Blossom.

"You did it!" Blossom squealed.

Beany nodded proudly. "It's easy when you know how," he quacked. "And we need to go this way. Follow me."

He flew to the gate at the edge of the field and waited for Blossom to squeeze underneath. Then he flew on, just a few feet above the ground. Blossom trotted after him. Beany flew up high sometimes

to make sure they were still going in the right direction.

Blossom watched her friend swoop and glide on his beautiful wings. She felt so proud of him. She watched and watched until her neck ached.

The path led into a dark and gloomy forest. Blossom lost sight of Beany among the trees. She began to feel very scared. The long shadows of the trees stretched across the ground, and the leaves rustled.

Blossom shivered. "Where are you, Beany?" she squealed in a very small voice.

Then she heard a loud quack. Beany swooped down beside her and stroked her back with his soft feathers.

"It's not far now," he quacked. He waddled beside her until the path left the woods and wound through the moonlit fields.

At last, the big barn came into sight. Blossom felt like cheering, but she was too tired. She had never walked so far in her life, and her feet were very sore.

Beany went as far as the gate of Blossom's field. He perched on the top rail, and this time he didn't wobble. He watched Blossom trot down toward the puddle. She pushed her way through the hedge and vanished into her own field.

It was past dinnertime, so Blossom headed straight back to her sty.

Her mother and all her brothers and sisters looked up from the trough when she arrived.

"Where have you been?" snorted her mom. "We were worried about you."

"I've been on an adventure," Blossom squealed.

"How could you have an adventure, just sitting in that puddle all day?" grunted her biggest brother.

"But I've been much farther than the puddle," Blossom told him proudly. She described what she had seen on her long walk.

"A big monster that gobbles up wheat?" grunted her biggest brother. "I don't believe you!"

"You couldn't have done all that on those short legs," snorted her second biggest brother.

"Don't pick on Blossom," scolded their mom. Then she looked at her littlest piglet. "I know you're a bit small," she snorted gently. "But you will grow. You shouldn't let your imagination run away with you."

"But I didn't imagine it," Blossom whispered to herself as she curled up in the straw. She decided that the next day she would take all her brothers and sisters to the farmyard to meet her friends. And to see the monster. She'd show them she was telling the truth!

Chapter Six

Beany stood beside the duck pond in the warm morning sun. He spread his dark brown wings and pointed his beak toward the sky. "I flew!" he quacked proudly to the other ducks. "I flew higher than the farmhouse and higher than the trees."

The other ducks listened and nodded their heads.

"My friend Blossom and I were lost," Beany continued. "I showed her the way home." He stopped. A familiar grunting noise was coming from the gate. Beany turned around and smiled. Blossom had come to see him!

"There she is now," Beany said, running down the track to meet her.

But it wasn't only Blossom who stood on the other side of the gate. Eleven other piglets were poking their little pink snouts through the bars. And eleven pairs of eyes were staring curiously at Beany.

"Hello!" quacked Beany.

Blossom wriggled under the gate. "Hi, Beany," she grunted. "I've brought my brothers and sisters to see you."

Beany watched as the other piglets began squeezing under the gate. They found the narrow space much more difficult to get through than Blossom did. At first, they all tried to get through at once. But they ended up with their legs all tangled together.

"One at a time," Blossom snorted.

At last, ten of the piglets had made it to the other side of the gate, which was all of them, except for Blossom's biggest brother. His plump pink tummy got stuck!

"You're too big," Blossom told him. She thought for a moment. "Hey! For once I'm not too small — you're too big!"

The biggest brother scratched at the ground with his feet until he'd dug a shallow hole. Even then he could *barely* squeeze through. "Phew!" he grunted breathlessly, shaking dust out of his ears.

Blossom led the litter of piglets up the track toward the farmyard and the duck pond. Beany waddled happily alongside her.

The other ducks crowded around to say hello to Blossom. But when they saw all the other piglets, they quacked and beat their wings in alarm.

"It's all right," Blossom squealed loudly. "These are my brothers and sisters. They won't hurt you."

But the ducks kept on quacking. Beany looked worriedly toward the farmhouse.

Mrs. Brown, the farmer's wife, might hear the noise and come out to see what was happening. Beany tried to calm down the ducks. But it was too late. The door opened.

"What's going on?" demanded Mrs. Brown, running outside. She stopped and looked amazed. "What are you piglets doing here, frightening my ducks? Go on! Shoo! Go back to your own field!"

Beany watched as Mrs. Brown shooed the piglets out of the farmyard and down the track. She opened the gate and herded through eleven little piglets.

Eleven?

Beany looked around the farmyard. Where was the missing piglet? He looked closely at an upside-down bucket. He could just see a pink snout poking out from one side and a curly tail from the other. It was Blossom. She had stayed behind.

As soon as Mrs. Brown had gone back inside, Blossom trotted out from her hiding place. "I'm not going home yet," she snorted to Beany. "Soon I'll be too big to squeeze under the gate, and I won't be able to visit you anymore." She looked down at her legs. "In fact, I think they've grown a bit already!"

Beany felt very happy for his friend. "I think you have, too," he agreed. "But don't forget, I can fly now! Even when you can't get under the gate, I'll always be able to fly over the hedge and visit you."

"So we can have lots more adventures!"
squealed Blossom happily.